GH00865565

Ruth loves to dance, act and tell stories. She was a teacher of English, Dance and Drama before coming to London to work for the Unicorn Theatre for children. Here she staged many children's community productions all over Westminster, including in the Cathedral. Ruth has travelled extensively taking groups of children to perform in World Theatre festivals where she has run workshops and told many stories. She continues to enjoy teaching through drama, story and dance. She has now found time to write her first book and hopes it will be the first of many.

Jill's Rocket Adventure

Adventure

Ruth Burgess

AUSTIN MACAULEY PUBLISHERS™

LONDON • CAMBRIDGE • NEW YORK • SHARJAH

A CIP catalogue record for this title is available from the British Library.

ISBN 9781398430068 (Paperback)
ISBN 9781398430075 (ePub e-book)

www.austinmacauley.com

First Published 2022
Austin Macauley Publishers Ltd®
1 Canada Square
Canary Wharf
London
E14 5AA

I would like to dedicate this book to the After School Drama Club children at the Convent of Jesus and Mary Infant school who helped to inspire its writing.

I would like to thank both family and close friends for their continued support and encouragement. In particular I give special thanks to Becky Cartwright for her input on illustrations and the feedback from her children, most useful. There are other numerous young people who read the first drafts and generously gave their feedback and suggestions for refining and improving for which I am very grateful. Particular thanks also to Sonia Jackman for pointing me in the right direction and giving invaluable advice.

Jill's Rocket Adventure By Ruth Burgess

Chapter One - The Day of the Launch

"Hand me that roll of cellotape," ordered Jill.

"Get it yourself," huffed Janet. She was tired of her sister ordering her about. She hadn't wanted to make a stupid boat from cardboard boxes anyway.

"Stop it you two," said Jenny, handing the cellotape to Jill to prevent any further quarrel. As the eldest sister she was always trying to keep the peace between her younger siblings.

"We'll need something for the wings," said Jill, sticking the edges of two bent and shaped boxes together to form the prow of the boat. "Why don't we go to dad's workshop and see what he's got, he may even be able to give us a hand by now, he promised he would when he'd finished his latest invention."

"He also said not to interrupt him and gave us all these bags of stuff to make something with for ourselves. There must be something we can use in one of them." Jenny started tipping out the contents of several bags of corks, plastic bottles, bottle tops, cardboard tubing, fabrics, wires and various other assorted goods that their dad had got from the local recycling centre. He was a regular customer of theirs.

Janet had decided to just lie on the grass in the shade of the tree and take a nap. She was upset that her idea of making a puppet theatre had been ditched in preference for a ridiculous flying boat, which was Jill's idea of course. How come the youngest always got their own way?

"Right, what are my three favourite princesses up to then on this glorious summer day?" asked Jack, their dad, as he came over to them.

"We're making a flying boat," said Jill proudly showing her dad what they'd done so far.

"But I don't think it'll go far as we don't have anything to make the wings from; a slight oversight on Jill's part I feel," whined Janet as she sat up and shaded her eyes from the sun.

"Not to worry I'm sure you'll find something," replied dad, tousling Janet's hair and smiling broadly.

"Can you help us dad?" asked Jill

"Soon, soon, I've nearly finished my latest project, I just wanted to get something from the shed so thought I'd pop over to see how things were going here," replied Jack.

"Can we lend you a hand dad?" asked Jenny.

"Er, very kind I'm sure but I'd rather you didn't, not after last time."

Last time they'd offered to paint his Jet Racer they'd ended up having a paint fight and getting sticky red paint all over each other. Jill declared it was all Janet's fault for spilling the paint in the first place and causing her to slip over in it.

"Let's not go over it now, all water, or red paint, under the bridge so to speak!" broke in Jenny before her sisters began yet another of their squabbles.

Jack sighed and ambled off towards the shed.

All three girls wondered what their father's latest invention was. Hopefully he'd let them in on the secret he'd been working on for the past year now he'd all but finished it, they each hoped for something different. Jenny, being the eldest, had wanted her own pair of Jet Wings since Jack had made the first prototype two years ago but had been told there were still refinements to be made. Janet had been pestering her father to make Jet Skis for their next skiing holiday - maybe they were ready now! Jill didn't really mind but whatever it was she wished she could have a hand in it.

Jack was coming back from the shed with a couple of bags and some tools.

"We'll carry those for you dad," offered Jenny.

"Well if you're sure you won't drop them," answered Jack with a meaningful look at Janet.

"We won't," Janet retaliated sharply.

They all walked over to the workshop that was a huge maze of warehouse style proportions, but just as they were about to go in Jack stopped, "Blast it I meant to bring the wire splicers and what with getting all that gear for your boat's wings I completely forgot about them."

"Shall I run back and get them for you dad?" offered Jill

"No, no, I can't remember where I left them, it'll be quicker if I go," said Jack as he turned to go back, "you go on in but don't touch anything and don't go into the Inner Chamber whatever you do," he shouted over his shoulder.

The girls smooched round looking at various drawings and diagrams of bicycles with wings, shoes with propellers, back packs with jet packs and various other ideas their dad was working on.

"I see he's still determined to invent something to do with transport," commented Janet.

"I wonder what made him so interested in this particular field of enquiry," pondered Jill.

"Well I think it would be a great idea to all have our own little Jet Packs, no more traffic jams, no more queuing for buses that never show up, and some independence. I'm all for it. Wonder what the big surprise is?" Asked Jenny.

"It must be near completion by now, dad's been working on it forever!" Janet sighed in exasperation.

"Yes well if it's to really work I expect it's a bit more complicated than sticking a few bits together and hoping for the best," replied Jill.

Jenny had wandered off to the far door, and although it said, "No Admittance" in bold type, she twisted the handle to see if it was locked. It wasn't. She ventured in, calling for the others to follow. They did. There was another door saying, "Positively No Entry". Again Jenny's hand reached for the handle and turned it, it gave way to another room. The girls stared about them, huge machines surrounded them on either side, but another door beckoned to them. It was painted bright red and bore the sign, "Inner Chamber. No Admittance on Pain of Death!!!" They were about to try the handle when Janet heard a scuffling noise behind her. She turned to see her father standing there. She coughed to try to let her sisters know but she was too late. Jenny's hand was already trying the door knob.

"Oh no you don't," came their father's roar. Jenny and Jill jumped around, their faces turning as scarlet as the door.

"What are you making in there dad, can't you tell us yet," asked Jill.

"Well I suppose there's no harm in telling you now I'm so near completion, come and take a peek," chuckled Jack.

Jack strode over to the inner chamber and unhooked a great big key which he slotted into the big metal door. The girls crowded up, pushing each other out of the way so that they should get first glimpse of this great secret.

"Ta Dah!" declared Jack as he threw the door wide to reveal his surprise.

"Wow,"

"Cor,"

"Blimey'" chorused the girls as they saw a gleaming pink and blue rocket standing on a jet plinth.

"Does that thing actually work, I mean will it take you up to space?" asked Jenny.

"I'm hoping it'll take me somewhere very special," was their father's reply.

"What do you mean dad, where?" asked Jill.

"Well a long time ago, when I was a little boy, about your age Jill, I accidentally grew some magic beans which went right up through the sky. I climbed them and found myself in Fairy Tale Land. Now I rather think it's time to go back."

"Go back, in that thing!" blurted out Jenny.

"Yes, you see there's someone there I need to say thank you to because they saved my life." Jack patiently continued.

"Saved your life?" repeated Jill.

"Yes, she was a Giantess and her husband kept wanting to eat me, but she hid me safely and fed him on other things so he forgot about the smell of me and when he fell asleep I could return safely."

"Weren't you scared?" asked Jenny.

"You bet I was, but I was also rather naughty, for every time I went I'd manage to escape with something belonging to the Giant, but his wife never gave me away. Then on my last visit I ran off with his harp but it sang out and woke the Giant who gave chase. I only just managed to get down the beanstalk in time and chop it down before he got down here too. He fell to the earth with such a crash you wouldn't believe and I'm afraid that was the end of him. But I couldn't get back up to fairy tale land ever again. I've been meaning to go back to the Giantess and thank her for her kindness but until now have never had the means to do so. Now I can put things right, if it's not too late." Jack poured out his story much to the girl's amazement. Who would have thought their father could have had such an adventure!

"That's fab dad, when will you go?" Jenny asked.

"Well I'm rather hoping to try it out as soon as I've made this last connection here," said their father pointing to a loose bit of cable and explaining where it had got to go. "I just need those wire splicers, but they didn't appear to be in the shed so I'm going to check in the other rooms. You can go inside and have a look around if you promise not to touch anything."

"We promise," answered Janet for all of them, and with that Jack set off back to the outer rooms.

Jenny and Janet stepped inside the rocket while Jill examined her father's circuitry. Then she saw the splicers her father needed just sitting there on the work bench. She decided to surprise her father by helping him out and fixing this final piece of wiring. She'd watched him many times so was confident she wouldn't make a mess of it. It was a relatively simple process. She took up the splicers and began to strip back the wires, following what her father had explained. While she was engaged in fixing things, Jenny and Janet were examining the levers, buttons and pulleys inside. They were careful not to touch anything but had strapped themselves into two seats and were imagining what it would be like to fly off to Fairy Tale Land when Jill came in wearing a big grin on her face.

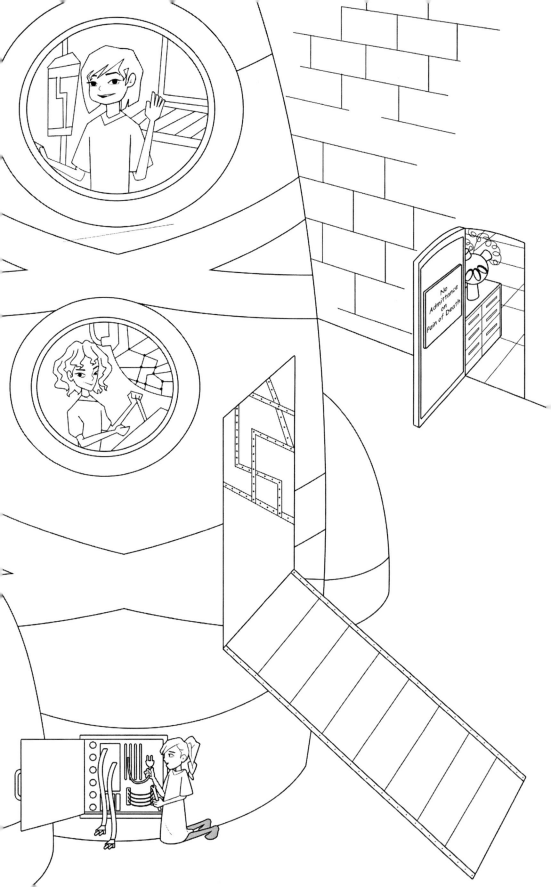

"All fixed," she announced.

"What's all fixed?" chorused Jenny and Janet together.

"The circuitry. I found dad's splicers and I've done the job for him as a nice surprise."

"Please tell me you haven't!" exclaimed Janet.

"What's wrong? I know what I'm doing I've watched dad often enough, I tell you I've done it." protested Jill.

"Dad'll go crazy when he finds out, we promised not to touch anything." argued Janet.

"You promised, I never said anything." Jill was quick to retort.

"Stop it you two," said Jenny, "I think I can hear dad coming back so it's too late we'll just have to face the music."

Now I don't know what caused it, maybe panic at the idea of their father's anger with them, but suddenly they all looked at each other and without a word began pressing buttons and pulling levers. Jill sat in the only other seat and strapped herself in. Before they knew it there was a clicking , clacking noise as the roof of the workshop opened above them. Then a tremendous roar as the engines ignited, then a burst of flame surrounded them and the girls began to panic, then an almighty jolt as the rocket shuddered into life and was launched into the air.

"Wow, we've only gone and done it. We're off on an adventure!" screamed Jill over the noise of the engines.

"Let's just hope it 's programmed to take us to Fairy Tale Land and nowhere else," commented Jenny.

"I just hope it'll get us back in one piece," said Janet.

Chapter Two – Welcome to Fairy Tale Land

Once they had got over the initial take off things settled down and the journey was just like any other flight they'd taken abroad, only a little more vertical!

"Wow, we've done it, we're going to Fairy Tale Land, I hope we can find the Giant's house and thank the Giantess for helping dad all those years ago," Jill piped up.

"She'll be pretty old by now," commented Jenny.

"We ought to have brought her something," said Janet.

"You're right, but then what could we possibly get for an old Giantess?" asked Jenny.

"Mmmm, perhaps we can find something when we get there," Jill chimed in.

"I don't think they have shops in Fairy Tale Land!" commented Janet sarcastically.

"How do you know, we've never been there so we might find anything," retorted Jill.

"Well we'll just have to wait and see won't we, no point in arguing about it," Jenny said quickly.

The journey continued in silence for a time, each girl keeping her thoughts to herself. There was a sudden juddering and vibrating that made all three girls tighten their seat belts and sit bolt upright.

"I think we're about to land," said jenny with a worried frown creasing her brow.

"Yep, here we go!" shouted Jill over the rumbling noises of the descending rocket.

"Hold on tight everyone," Jenny ordered.

Down they went. Down, down, down, until finally there was a scraping sound as the rocket bumped to a standstill on a rough patch of ground.

"I feel sick," groaned Janet, "all that bumping and shaking."

"Stop moaning, we're here aren't we, let's get out and take a look around. I can't wait to see what it's like." Jill was already out of her seat and racing towards the rocket door.

"Wait a minute, let's just check out of the window first before we stumble headlong into something we're not prepared for," warned Jenny sensibly.

"What could there possibly be?" queried Jill, slightly cross at being stopped.

"Oh, I don't know; how about wolves, evil witches and wizards and fire breathing dragons for starters! Or had you forgotten that Fairy Tales have evil characters as well as good?" came the swift reply from Janet.

Jill stopped in her tracks as she realized the truth behind this, every Fairy Story she'd heard had its dark side, perhaps it was best if they took a look out the window first.

They clambered up to where a small window looked out and would give them their first view of this magical land.

"Is that what I think it is?" asked Janet pointing to the left.

"It's a house of sorts, but not like any I've seen and certainly not big enough for a Giant to live in." said Jenny.

"Looks like it's covered in sweets, great stuff, I'm starving, looks like we've found lunch!" said Jill cheerfully.

"Aren't you forgetting something Jill, as always!" pointed out Janet.

"What, don't tell me you don't want to taste those sweets!" exclaimed Jill.

"Not if it means being dinner for a witch, no! Don't you remember Hansel and Gretel?" Janet replied impatiently.

"Ah, yes, slipped my mind for a moment, thanks Janet" said Jill contritely.

"But hold on a moment Gretel tricked the witch into the oven didn't she and then got away, so that must mean the house is empty", declared Jill in triumph.

"Not necessarily, someone else might have moved in," said Janet defiantly. "Okay, we need a plan," put in Jenny, "we have to establish whether there's a witch or someone else living there. "

After thinking for a while the girls hatched a plan together. They would simply follow Gretel's example and trick the witch, if there was one. First they must establish if there was a witch or not.

Once outside the girls tiptoed softly across the grass to one of the side windows. They peered inside and saw a woman sitting in a rocking chair, wrapped in a witch's cloak, fortunately with her eyes closed. They dipped back down below the window sill. Jenny signaled for them to be quiet. They crawled back to the rocket as quietly as they could.

"I knew it, you see there is a witch and we're all going to get fattened up and eaten, it's all your fault Jill," said a frightened Janet.

"Let's not panic, she might not see us," replied a shaky Jill.

"But I rather think she'll spot a bright pink rocket in the middle of her garden, don't you?" Janet said sarcastically.

"Now, now, remember we've got a plan, and there's no time to waste, so pick up those shovels you two and let's get cracking. Quickly now, she might wake up any time soon." Jenny calmly handed her sisters a spade each and they followed her quickly behind the rocket and started to dig. Fortunately the ground was soft and they'd soon made a deep hollow and begun tunneling under the ground towards the witch's house. As they got closer they could smell the chocolate that the house was made of and Jill couldn't resist taking a bite, then another and another. Yummy! Her sisters were quick to follow her example, and soon they were all giggling and stuffing their faces, which were now covered in chocolate.

They must have been right under the witch's living room for suddenly, they heard the screech of a chair being moved and footsteps above them. Uh,uh, this could be trouble. They began digging more earnestly than ever. Now they heard a cackle of a laugh and a door slamming. Oh no the witch knew she had visitors, how long would it take her to find them?

"Quick we have to eat our way through," ordered Jenny.

"But I'll be sick if I eat any more," said Jill.

"It was your idea remember, so get eating," snarled Janet as she shoveled another mouthful in.

As they dug and ate they heard the witch stomping about above them, clearly searching for intruders. Then they heard her leave the house. They knew she would find the tunnel entrance any time soon and be after them. There was no time to loose.

Just then a mouse appeared, Janet screamed and Jenny clamped her hand over her sister's mouth.

The mouse spoke, "Can I be of assistance, you seem to be in a bit of trouble, and if you'll forgive me saying so, you're making a right old mess of this tunnel you're digging."

Jill was the quickest to recover her wits and manners and quickly explained what they were attempting.

"Oh dear, Oh dear, you'll never do it, not this way anyway. Would you like some help? I have some very good friends, all expert tunnelers, perhaps I should give them a call," offered the mouse.

"Why, yes please!" said the girls with relief.

Within moments the mouse had rustled up a team of creatures from badgers and moles to mice, rats and rabbits, all of whom seemed willing to help with the digging.

Mole could smell the way forward and clear to the boundary with the wood and Badger offered to guide them through the forest once they were safely away.

Jenny was bringing up the rear and could sense the witch was now entering the tunnel, she urged everyone to dig faster than ever. As the chocolate was passed down the line to her she built up a wall behind her, hoping to delay the witch and buy them a bit more time. They were certainly making better progress now they had help.

Suddenly there was a ray of light, they'd come up the other side of the house into the woods. Everyone scurried up the tunnel and out into the daylight as fast as they could, except Mole who said he'd rather make his way underground if there was no objection. They thanked him and waved goodbye as he nosed back down into the depths of the tunnel once more. The rabbits said they'd better follow and lend him a paw in blocking off the tunnel so that the witch couldn't follow and with that jumped down the hole one after the other, waving a paw as they did so.

The Mice and Rats made their apologies but said they'd better be off too as they had families to feed and look out for and they scattered in every direction through the woods. That left the girls with Badger who asked, "What brings you to these parts anyway, you're too young to be wandering a dangerous place like this all on your own, ain't you got no parents?"

"We've come to visit the Giantess, to thank her on our father's behalf for looking after him when he was a boy," answered Jenny.

"The Giantess? Looked after your father you say? Would that be young Jack then, I remember hearing stories of a young lad who tricked the Giant out of his fortune, that wouldn't be your father would it?" Badger enquired.

"The one and the same," said Jill proudly.

"Is it far from here, where the Giantess lives?" asked Janet.

"Well now, that depends on which way you go," replied Badger.

"If you could direct us by the quickest route we'd be most grateful," said Jenny politely.

"Well now it would be quickest to go over the river by the bridge but there's a Troll who's not too keen on letting people pass so you might be better off going down river further, crossing by the stepping stones and then making your way back up, only then you'll like as not meet the wolf. I'm afraid whichever way you go is fraught with danger of delay," mused Badger.

"Never mind, we'll find a way," said Jill cheerfully, "just lead us to the river if you will please Mr. Badger."

"Why this way then young ones," said Badger as he began to walk through the trees.

Chapter Three – Crossing the River

After tumbling through the woods, tripping over roots and getting thorns in their legs the girls arrived at the river, thanked Badger for all his help and were ready to continue their journey. They just had to get past the Troll who guarded the bridge or risk an encounter with a wolf who liked to eat children.

"I think we'd better take the long way round and hope we don't meet the wolf," said Jenny.

"But if we cross the bridge at least we know what we're dealing with and can prepare ourselves," said Jill thoughtfully.

"Can't we just go back home and forget all this nonsense," protested Janet.

"No, certainly not," chimed Jenny and Jill together.

"Well I don't want to be picked off by the wolf, I remember what big eyes he has, big ears too and as for those teeth, well…."

"All the better to eat you with!" chanted Jenny and Jill.

"It's not funny," sulked Janet.

"Alright looks like we'd better cross the bridge and face the Troll then," agreed Jenny.

"How did the three Billy Goats Gruff do it?" asked Jill

"Well the youngest went first and told of a bigger brother behind, so the Troll let him go, then the middle one went trip trapping across and again said there was a bigger brother still to come so again the Troll let him go. Then the eldest and biggest goat went onto the bridge and said he wasn't afraid of the Troll and if he wanted to eat him he'd better come and get him, and when he did the goat lowered his head and butted him with his horns right off the bridge and into the river below," explained Janet.

"Oh yes I remember now, it made me laugh when I saw the mean and nasty Troll being head butted. We should do the same, I'll go first, then you Janet, then Jenny," suggested Jill.

"Aren't you forgetting something – I don't have horns!" exclaimed Jenny. "How am I supposed to wrestle with a mean and nasty Troll who wants to eat me!

"Ah, good point," admitted Jill. "How about you trick him into the river by telling him you've seen a really big fish or something?"
"It's a bit risky isn't it, I mean what if he doesn't believe me?" came Jenny's worried reply.
"Mmm, I suppose it's not really fair to leave you to face him on your own," admitted Jill.
"Seems perfectly alright to me," said Janet.

"No, we're in this together, so we should stick together. That's it – stick together! We could join up into one big monster like creature and scare him. I could balance on Jenny's shoulders and Janet you can hold on behind Jenny to make us look really big,"
Jill was in full throw of her new idea when Janet cut her off, " I see, I get to play the back end of a Monster, charming I'm sure!"
"We'll need something to cover us up and look Monster like but there's all sorts of reeds and rushes we could weave together into a cloak or something," Jill continued enthusiastically.

"Well it's certainly a better idea than me facing him on my own, any other suggestion Janet?" asked Jenny.
"Well no, but I don't like it all the same!" said Janet.

"Come on, let's see what we can find to cover us up with," shouted Jill as she rushed down to the water's edge.

Her sisters joined her and soon they were busy pulling and tugging at grasses and reeds and weaving them together as best they could. It took them the best part of the day to complete something that looked big enough, but eventually the job was done.

Then Janet insisted they rehearse, she liked directing plays and was always creating little performances. She saw this as their most challenging performance yet, which it was, because if they didn't get it right the Troll would surely eat them.

Jenny struggled to get Jill up on her shoulders but after collapsing in heaps of laughter a few times they finally managed it. Janet had them practicing their lines until she was happy they knew what they were doing and Jill had put on her deepest and meanest voice. Then Janet threw the cloak of reeds over them, she had to admit it did lend an air of River Monster to them which she was quite happy with. She adjusted the cloak so that Jenny could see through the slits they'd made and then took up her position behind her and they began to creep along the river bank towards the distant bridge. Jenny nearly slipped a couple of times and they very nearly all ended up in the river.

Soon the bridge loomed up in front of them and Jenny felt her tummy do somersaults at what they were about to do. Janet was gripping on behind her and followed blindly in Jenny's wake oblivious of how near they were to their fate, which was just as well or she might have ditched the whole idea and run away. Jill sat majestically atop Jenny's shoulders, wearing a wreath of thorny bush for some kind of head-dress. She appeared un-phased by the prospect of meeting the Troll, in fact she was clearly enjoying the whole thing.

Now came the moment of truth, Jenny took her first step tentatively onto the bridge. Then the next and the next, nothing happened. Perhaps the Troll had gone, or was asleep under the bridge with a full belly and wouldn't be venturing out to eat them after all. They took another three steps and then came a rumbling, jostling and shaking which nearly made Jenny loose her footing once more, but she grasped the rail and steadied herself just in time. Then came the Troll's booming voice, " Who's that trip trapping across my bridge?"

Before them stood the ugliest looking Troll you could imagine, sporting a bald head with hairy warts popping out all over it, beady little eyes of piercing blue, a large bulbous nose that was bright red in colour and thin mean lips from where hung a lolloping tongue with which he licked up the spittle that dribbled down his pointy chin. He wore a rainbow coloured rag jacket over patchwork knee length trousers that showed his knobbly knees peeking out below. On his feet were big hobnail boots. He was as broad as he was tall but Jill still seemed to tower over him.

"It is I, the mighty River Monster. Who stands in my way? Let me pass or you will regret it." Jill's voice boomed out impressively.

"But I've always stood sentry on this bridge and controlled who passes," the Troll protested.

"But I control the river and all that crosses it is mine," Jill answered swiftly. "You may continue to live under the bridge only if I say so."

"I am hungry and you would make a good meal," the Troll said refusing to back down.

Jill had to think on her feet, or rather on Jenny's shoulders, "I taste of rotten fish and will make you ill if you eat me, so don't even think about it!"

"Ugh, very well I will let you pass if you allow me to stay here as before," bargained the Troll.

"Let us pass then Troll and you will have control once more," Jill's voice roared.

The Troll stood to one side and Jenny strode out with a wibble and wobble as she balanced Jill and supported the half fainted Janet across the bridge and came safely to the other side.

The Troll had jumped back down and ducked under the cover of the bridge ready to surprise the next unsuspecting river crosser and the girls kept up their disguise until they were well and truly out of sight of the bridge.

Jill shrugged off the cloak, Janet clambered out weak kneed from under, and Jenny fell down exhausted. Then they all looked at each other and laughed. They'd done it! They were jubilant. They were one step closer to finding the Giant's castle.

Chapter Four – Meeting the Gingerbread Man

Once they'd got their breath back the girls scrambled to their feet and took a look around them to get their bearings. Badger had told them they needed to head East, but which way was that?

" I think the sun rises in the East and sets in the West," said Janet helpfully, "Or is it the other way round. I'm not sure!"

"Well whichever way we go seems to be pretty hilly," observed Jill.

"Let's get to the top of that hill and see if we can get a better view," suggested Jenny as she pointed to the hill ahead.

It was quite a trek and soon the girls were panting for breath, but they were nearing the summit at last. Jill found a hidden reserve of energy and sprinted to the top, "More hills, just endless hills," she shouted down to her sisters who were slowly plodding towards her.

"Yes you're right," panted Jenny as she surveyed the land before them.

"I can't go another step," said Janet as she flopped to the ground beside them.

"It'll be easier going down," chirped Jill brightly, "We can roll down. Race you!"

With that she lay down and began to roll down the hill, Jenny and Janet watched for a moment but it did look fun and so a second later they were joining her on a downward roll, all tiredness forgotten. It was bumpy ground and they bounced over the bumps, getting giddier and giddier as they went.

"Wow, that was fun!" exclaimed Jill on reaching the bottom, "almost made the climb worth while."

"Good job we didn't have to carry a pail of water like your namesake," giggled Janet, "or we'd have spilt it all over the place!"

"But seriously, which way should we go now?" asked Jenny as she brushed grass from her trousers, and ran her fingers through her hair to comb out any stray grass that might have got stuck there.

"Onwards and upwards seems the only option," said Jill as she took a deep breath and looked around her.

"Hold on what's that, over there?" asked Janet as she pointed up the hill slightly to the left of them.

"Where?" asked Jenny.

"There seems to be something moving over there on that hill and it's coming down in our direction," replied Janet.

The girls squinted into the sunlight and sure enough they began to make out a funny little shape running and rolling down the hill.

Then Janet noticed other shapes appearing over the brow of the hill, "There's more of them giving chase behind."

"Perhaps we should run too, they might be being chased by a wolf or a witch or worse!" said Jenny as she turned to head back up the hill they'd just descended.

"No, no, wait!" shouted Jill, "I think I can make out who or what it is, look!" The girls peered into the distance and sure enough the first shape was getting closer and they could make out arms and legs jutting out in rather a splayed out fashion for one intent on running so fast.

"I do believe it's the Gingerbread Man!" exclaimed Janet.

"Yes, yes, it is, isn't he funny," chuckled Jill.

"He must be running because that crowd behind him want to eat him, just like in his story," said Janet.

"How awful, being constantly chased, he must be exhausted, perhaps we should help him," suggested Jill.

"But how?" asked Jenny.

"I don't know, but we need to put the chasing crowd off eating him somehow," stated Jill.

"But he smells so delicious I'm not surprised everyone wants to eat him, I would too," commented Janet.

"That's it then, we must make him smell awful so that no-one wants to eat him. Well done Janet." Jenny praised her sister and then started rummaging through her rucksack to see what she could find that smelt rotten. Out came her hairbrush, make-up bag, purse, mobile phone, water bottle, pen, and various other bits and bobs that Jenny considered important enough to travel with her wherever she went. "Nothing here, have either of you got anything?" she asked.

"I've got a pair of smelly old socks," offered Jill, waving them in-front of Jenny's nose.

"Don't be silly, we need something to spray all over him, how about this perfume of mine," offered Janet, "it's pretty smelly and you certainly wouldn't want to eat it."

"Excellent idea," agreed Jenny.

The Gingerbread Man was coming at full pelt towards them, they weren't sure whether he'd seen them or not so they began to jump up and down and wave their arms in the air. This only served to make him put the brakes on and come to a skidding halt. Perhaps he thought they'd want to eat him too. He was looking over his shoulder to the crowd who were gaining ground on him, then he seemed to make a decision and came on again towards the girls. Behind him came an old woman waving her stick at him, a ginger cat wearing thigh length boots, a little girl in a bright red cloak, a cow and a dancing spoon.

The Gingerbread Man arrived at their feet.

"Hi, you must be the Gingerbread Man, I'm Jill."

"Have you just tumbled down that hill then?" asked the Gingerbread Man on arrival.

"Erm, yes, but how did you know that?"

"Well you're always doing it aren't you? Isn't Jack with you today?"

"No, he's at home and doesn't actually know we're here," said a confused Jill.

"Still nursing his sore head is he?" continued the Gingerbread Man.

"He hasn't actually got a sore head. Though I expect he's nursing a headache with us three having shot off in his rocket."

"I think there's a little bit of confusion here," butted in Jenny, "I'm Jenny and these are my sisters, Janet and Jill. We've come to find the Giantess and thank her on our father's behalf for saving his life back when he was a little boy."

"The Giantess you say, well you won't find her in these hills, she lives miles away on the other side of Fairy Tale Land. I'd give you some directions but I'm being chased by some rather hungry folk as you can see and must be on my way if I'm to avoid being eaten. Excuse me, won't you." The Gingerbread Man made to run off but Janet made a grab for his outreached hand and held on to him.

"Not so fast little man, we could do with every bit of help we can get so if we get rid of your followers will you promise to help us in return?"

"Why certainly, but there's no time to loose, they'll be upon us any second now so do let me go and we can all run up that hill and be on our way."

"We've got a better idea, just stand still and let us spray you with this perfume and the smell will stop them wanting to eat you."

"Are you sure?"

"As sure as anyone can be about such things."

With that Janet began to spray the perfume all over the Gingerbread Man. He gasped and spluttered and coughed and nearly choked on the fumes but there was no trace of ginger by the time the job was finished, instead a heavy cloying aroma of some flower filled the air around him. His pursuers were now closing in and Janet stepped aside allowing them to come within smelling distance.

The old woman who was leading the way took in a full gasp and then her eyes watered and she blinked several times before reeling and finally falling backwards into the Puss in Boots, who in turn crashed backwards into Little Red Riding Hood, who stumbled and tripped knocking over the Cow, who almost swallowed the Spoon! What a sight they were!

There followed an almighty row as they scrambled to their feet each blaming another for their misfortune.

Jenny, Janet and Jill stood by and watched with amused grins spread across their faces. It seemed the perfume smells were so overpowering they'd all but forgotten what it was that had brought them to this predicament.

"I think you'll be safe until the perfume wears off," said Janet, "and try not to get wet or it'll wash off."

"Well it certainly seems to have done the trick," admitted the Gingerbread Man, "I don't suppose I could have that spray, to keep it handy if ever a top up is required?"

"You most certainly can," offered Jill, taking it out of Janet's hands and offering it to him.

"Why thank you most kindly," replied the Gingerbread Man as he reached out to take it.

"Hold on a minute, not so fast," said Janet as she knocked his hand out of the way, "First you must tell us the way to the Giantess's castle, you promised remember."

"Why yes of course, I had every intention of doing so," answered the Gingerbread Man.

So it was that the girls learnt that they had to go over two more hills and then bare right, which apparently was East and they'd see a cave running through the big mountain, they should make for that.

Chapter Five – An Encounter with a Spider

By the time the girls reached the big mountain it was getting dark and the full moon was glowing in the darkening sky. Now if they could just find the entrance to the cave they'd at least have some shelter for the night ahead.

"There doesn't look like there's an entrance to me," moaned Janet, "If that Gingerbread man has been spinning us a tale and this is the wrong way we could be in grave danger."

"Why would he do that, we helped him didn't we," Jill said confidently.

"But he's just a biscuit, who ever heard of trusting a bis….!" Janet started to reply.

"Well I for one thought he was a decent enough fellow," Jenny butted in firmly, "so let's not waste time arguing but get on with looking for a way in. Jill you go that way and Janet and I will go this."

Janet thought about digging her heels in and refusing but decided it was easier to go along with Jenny. Jill set off in the opposite direction. They were feeling their way round the stubbly mountain base hoping to come across a gaping hole or even a narrow crack of an opening, but the mountain stood solid giving no sign of an entrance. Janet sat down on a broken bit of rock about to protest that it was all a waste of time and they might as well go home, when they heard a shriek of delight from Jill.

"Over here, quick I've found it!"

Jenny grabbed Janet's hand, hauled her up from the rock and they began jogging back round the mountain till they came upon Jill standing outside a dark portal that led into the mountain.

"This must be it," said Jill, "Come on let's go in." With that she disappeared into the mountain before either of her sisters could utter a word of warning. They followed more slowly, wishing they had a torch to shine some light upon their way. The walls were wet and slimy with lichen, the floor uneven and the dark got more intense the further in they ventured.

Janet began to whimper, "I don't like it in here, can we please go back outside."

"We're probably safer in here, at least it doesn't smell like wolves or monsters have been using it as a lair," reassured Jill.

"And that's supposed to reassure me is it! How about creepy crawlies, I expect there's hundreds of them, or we could be wondering right into a bat cave, and there's probably rats too. I hate all those things."

"They're not likely to do you much harm though are they, and if you can't see them you won't know they're there and you can just walk straight past them. If you'd got a torch, the light would bring them out and you'd see them so there'd be more to be scared of," Jill reasoned.

"But I know they're there and if I can't see them I might put my hand on them or step on one and hear it crunch under my foot."

"Well then it would be dead and you'd have nothing to worry about would you!"

"Orghh, you're impossible!" Janet gave in and continued following. She certainly didn't want to be on her own and at least while she'd been arguing she hadn't noticed the scurrying claws that tracked across the passageway where they trod.

Jenny suddenly stopped and squirmed in-front of them both, "Yuck," she declared, "I think I just walked through a spider web, it's all sticky on my face."

"What did I tell you," said Janet as she shuddered at the thought.

"Well if Jenny's got it on her face, then the way ahead is clear for you, or perhaps you'd like to lead the way," challenged Jill.

"No way, I'll stick to bringing up the rear," answered Janet nervously.

They pushed on, deeper and deeper into the heart of the mountain until suddenly there seemed to be more air; they'd arrived at some sort of cavern within the mountain.

"I don't know about you two but I'm done in. How about we sleep here for the night," Jenny suggested.

"Sleep? I couldn't sleep if I tried, just the thought of all those nasty bugs makes my skin crawl, how can you think of sleep?" asked Janet incredulously.

"Well you can keep watch if you like but I'm with Jenny, it's been a long and exhausting day and I could certainly use some shut eye." With that Jill sat herself down with her back to the rock, wriggled about for a while until, finally comfortable, she closed her eyes and soon fell fast asleep.

"Wake us if there's anything life threatening," yawned Jenny as she joined Jill in getting as comfortable as she could on the hard rock floor.

"It's not fair," mumbled Janet as she too dropped to the floor and stared about her. Her eyes had become accustomed to the dark and she could make out vague shapes that her imagination turned into all sorts of frightening images. What she didn't know was that way above them, clinging to the roof of the cavern, was a giant spider who'd been listening in to all the girl's talk. He rather prided himself on being scary – he'd frightened Little Miss Muffet right off her tuffet, but that had been a long time ago, and now he saw another opportunity to have some fun. He began spinning his silk into a long rope to abseil down. When it was long enough he silently clambered down until he dropped right in-front of Janet's face. Her eyes were just beginning to close, her body to relax and sleep take over when she saw the huge spider before her. She screamed. Loudly. Jenny and Jill both shot up, awake in an instant.

"What is it, what is it?" they asked.

"A gi.., gi.., ginormous spider," squeaked Janet, who could barely bring herself to speak.

"Hee, hee, seems I've glued this one to the seat," chuckled the spider.

"Why hello, Mr. Spider, charmed to meet you. You are a handsome fellow aren't you?" said Jill getting into her stride and peering closely at the spider. "What a fine bit of spinning you've done."

"Why thank you. No-one normally takes the time or trouble to see the workmanship involved in spinning a rope or web, and no-one's ever called me handsome before!" replied the spider.

"Would you be kind enough to step onto my hand here, so that I can get a better look at you. You're making my sister nervous you see, she doesn't understand the beauty of nature sometimes, but perhaps if I could show her you're not dangerous she might even come to like you."

"Why I'd be honoured," said the spider as he crawled onto Jill's outstretched hand.

With the spider removed Janet began to cry with relief and Jenny went swiftly to her side to give her a big hug and whispered that it was all alright now.

Meanwhile the Spider and Jill were deep in conversation, swapping stories of their adventures, their families and everything else besides.

Once Jill had explained the reason for their being there the Spider insisted on escorting them through the tunnels of the mountain and safely out the other side.

Even Janet was prepared to trust him now she knew him better and found herself conversing with him quite normally as they made their way and thereby forgetting all the scary things that might be lurking in the dark.

They soon reached another opening and blinked as the sunlight greeted them.

"Thank you kindly Mr. Spider," said Jill, "It's been a pleasure meeting you."

"The pleasure's all mine," said the Spider, "and I hope you've forgiven me for that little prank of mine, can we be friends?" Spider turned and offered a leg to Janet, who took it gently between finger and thumb and gave it a little shake.

"Why yes, I do believe we can," she said smiling to herself in disbelief that this was really happening.

Chapter Six – Through Field and Forest

With their eyes adjusted to the morning sun, the girls came out of the mountain and looked about them. There were green fields, some woods in the distance, some crops growing in fields, sheep and cows in others. They wondered what this leg of the journey would have in store for them.

They set off towards a field with sheep in it, as they seemed less threatening than the cows, who might after all be Bulls Janet decided. Once in the muddy field they followed a worn path that cut across the middle of the field. The sheep turned to stare at them as they went and a couple of them started to follow them, baa-ing noisily as they did so. More sheep were attracted by the noise and so they began to follow too, until soon all the sheep seemed to be following them across the field.

"We seem to have attracted a crowd," said Jenny.

"They probably think we're farmers or shepherds or something," added Janet.

"That one looks a bit different," said Jill pointing to one with a black little face and white fluffy coat. "He's rather cute isn't he?"

"He'd probably taste nice with a bit of mint sauce," laughed Janet.

"How could you! I'll never eat lamb again," Jill said.

"Bet you do, as soon as we get home and forget all this, you'll be back demanding the biggest chicken leg, bacon and eggs for breakfast, sausage and chips for tea, and a tasty slice of roast lamb come the Sunday roast," Jenny was quick to point out.

"I think we've got company," whispered Janet.

A little girl in a flouncy blue dress was clambering over a gate at the other end of the field. She wore a pretty little blue bonnet too and carried a shepherd's crook. She seemed to be waving at them so the girls waved back. As they got closer they could see that she was frowning and far from happy.

"Did you steal my sheep?" she asked sharply.

"I beg your pardon but we haven't stolen any sheep," replied Jenny.

"Well that one there with the black face is mine and I've been looking for her all morning," said the little girl in blue.

"Well we were just crossing the field and the sheep followed us, we had no idea whose they were I'm afraid," continued Jenny.

"What are you doing here anyway? The farmer won't be happy that you're tramping all over his land."

"We're on our way to see the Giantess to thank her for saving our father," explained Janet.

"Oh I wouldn't be going there if I were you," advised the little girl.

"Why not?" chipped in Jill.

"Well besides her being so huge, they say that now she's old she's very grumpy, has lost her sight, can't hear very well and the only good thing is that she has very few teeth to chew with," the girl explained.

"Sounds like she could do with a friendly visit and perhaps a nice bunch of flowers to cheer her up. Maybe we should get her a pair of glasses, hearing aid and false teeth too," Jenny said defensively.

"Now where would you get a pair of glasses big enough for a Giant?" laughed the little girl.

"I really don't know, but maybe we'll find somewhere on our journey," said Jenny hopefully.

"Well I can take you into the town if you like, but first I have to go into the woods where Hare and Tortoise are having another of their races. I don't know how Tortoise keeps winning, but he does, and I don't want to miss how he tricks Hare this time."

"Sounds like fun, can we join you?" Jill was quick to ask.

"Well looks like my sheep has taken a fancy to you, whereas she keeps running away from me, so it would be helpful I suppose," Mary, the little girl decided, "Come on, this way."

She set off back to the gate and the girls followed her, closely followed by the sheep.

As they walked Mary told the girls how her sheep used to follow her everywhere, even going to school with her, though that didn't meet with the teacher's approval, who wouldn't allow it into the classroom. Eventually the sheep had grown bored with waiting for her every day and so started to go off on long walks and now hardly followed her at all.

"Oh, I'm sorry," said Jenny, "But he seems to be following us alright now."

"Yes, he likes to skip about in the woods, I do too." With that she began to skip along and the girls found themselves jogging to keep up.

Before they realized it they were deep in a thick forest of trees where a crowd seemed to be gathering, there were ducks, pigs, bears, squirrels, mice and all sorts of towns folk, all with cameras or mobiles at the ready.

"What's going on?" asked Jill.

"A race between Hare and Tortoise," answered Janet, "don't you ever listen!"

"But why has everyone got cameras?" persisted Jill.

"I don't know, but get your mobile ready for whatever it is," whispered Janet.

"Okay, okay!"

There was a lot of chatter and laughter from the crowd who didn't seem to notice the three girls who were doing their best to blend in with those around them.

Suddenly the crowd went quiet, Tortoise had arrived.

"Welcome everyone, thank you all for coming out. I hope you've all brought a camera of sorts with you. I've called you all here early to ask for your help in getting me to win this race again. You all know how boastful Hare can be and I just want to teach him a lesson." Tortoise's voice was deep and slow and everyone was listening carefully to what he had to say.

"Now if you could hide yourselves along the route of the race and pop out with your cameras and get Hare to pose for some photos, or even interview him or get his autograph, and so delay him it might just give me enough time to get past him and pip him to the post. He's so proud he's sure to want his photo taken, unless he's learnt his lesson from last time, but I somehow doubt it." Tortoise went on to direct some of the crowd into hiding places so that they wouldn't all come out at once. Mary and the girls, and the little black nosed sheep of course, walked towards the end of the course and took cover amongst the trees.

Tortoise left everyone in position and then ambled back to the starting point. He hadn't long to wait before Hare turned up wearing a big grin across his face.

"You're not going to trick me today," he said confidently, "I won't be stopping for dinner this time, I made sure I had lunch earlier so I won't be tempted. So now we'll see who's really the fastest, though we hardly have to race to prove that it's obviously me!" he boasted.

Puss in Boots was there to start the race fairly. He got them to stand side by side, then raising his hat in the air he called, "Ready, steady, go!" bringing his hat smartly down and so the race began.

Hare sprinted ahead leaving Tortoise well behind. Just round the first bend, three blind mice tumbled onto the race track in-front of Hare.

"Oh Hare, you're so fast, please can we have your autograph?" they asked, running round his legs and very nearly tripping him up.

"Autograph, why yes of course. Have you got paper and pen?"

"Er, no, but sign the back of this leaf, I'm sure that will do," said one of the mice as he felt around for a broad leaf.

"There's some mud for your paw just a little off the track over here," said another.

"So kind of you Hare, we do so admire you," said the third.

Hare was flattered. He bounced off the track and into the woods, following the mice who were beginning to run round in circles each shouting,

"This way,"

"Just a little further,"

"Over here Hare,"

They were leading him a merry dance around the woods until they'd somehow managed to get him back to the start of the race and he found himself behind Tortoise. Hare quickly put his front paw into a muddy puddle and then printed his mark on the back of the leaf. He was still confident that with a few good bounds he could be back in-front again.

Tortoise took no notice of any of the commotion and carried steadily on, head down, carrying his shell. Hare came bounding past once more ahead. He laughed, "You'll never win Tortoise, I'm far too fast!"

Just ahead three pigs crossed his path. Hare came to a screeching halt.

"Here he is!" shouted one of the pigs, "I knew he'd be winning."

"Can we have your photo?" asked a second.

"You'll still win, you've plenty of time," assured the third.

Hare couldn't resist, "Very well," he said as he took up a winner's pose for the cameras pointed at him.

"Click, click," went the Three Little Pigs, as they asked him to turn this way and that to get his best side.

They kept this up just long enough for Tortoise to catch up and sneak ahead once more.

"I don't believe it, how did you get ahead?" exclaimed Hare when he saw Tortoise out along the path in-front of him.

"Still it won't matter, a couple of jumps and I'll be back in the lead in no time."

Sure enough he streaked ahead in no time, but only to find himself being stopped by another enthusiastic group of fans, wanting photos, autographs and even a chat and some advice.

One of five little Ducks wanted to know if Hare could swim as well as he could run. Another asked if he had any brothers or sisters. The third wanted to know if his mother or father had taught him how to run so fast, and the fourth asked if he ever got lost in the forest. The fifth was rather shy and just took his photo.

Hare answered the questions as best he could and posed for his picture to be taken, all of which took so long, you've guessed it, Tortoise had caught up and over taken Hare once more.

This pattern was repeated several more times until they reached the final leg of the race. Tortoise had kept up a slow but steady pace and wasn't in the least bit tired, but Hare had been led a merry dance and been bounding all over the forest and so was fast tiring and showing signs of slowing down. He was almost glad to take a break and catch his breath when it came to Mary and the three girls turn to play their part in Tortoise's clever trick.

Mary stepped out, "Excuse me Hare could you spare a moment to talk to these three reporters who want to do an article about you for a magazine that will be read by millions?"

"Oh, fame at last, I knew my celebrity status would grow. Where are you from? I don't recognize you from around here?"

"We're from back down on Earth, we've come by rocket, and we'd love to get your story for the people back home," said Jenny, catching on to Mary's idea quickly.

"Wow, that's just great, international fame at last. Nothing more than I deserve of course!" Hare announced proudly.

"if we could just draw you to the side here so we can record you on tape without the background noise," put in Jill as she beckoned him off the track and into a quieter spot.

"Why, certainly, certainly," said Hare as he followed the girls.

The girls proceeded to conduct an interview with Hare for as long as it took for Tortoise to get well enough ahead that he was assured of winning.

Mary gave them a signal when it was safe for them to wind the interview up and with a few last shots of Hare grinning from ear to ear they concluded their interview and led Hare back to the track.

Hare of course thought he was still ahead of Tortoise and so didn't rush, but when he reached the final home strait, there was Tortoise waiting for him! He couldn't believe it, how had that happened again, perhaps Tortoise wasn't as slow as he imagined.

There was a huge crowd, all laughing and cheering for Tortoise and those three reporters were there too taking more pictures and interviewing Tortoise, who'd now get all the glory and fame. Hare hung his head down low and skulked off into the forest before anyone got a chance to see his disappointment.

"Well done Tortoise, that should stop him from ever challenging you again, you've certainly proved that speed isn't always needed to win a race!" said Jenny.

"Isn't it time we got on our way?" asked Janet.

"Where are you going?" enquired Tortoise.

"To see the Giantess," answered Jill.

"Oh the Three Little Pigs are going in her direction, I'm sure they'll be happy to accompany you," assured Tortoise.

Chapter Seven – The Three Little Pigs and the Big Bad Wolf

Indeed they were! They were glad mainly because the girls would offer them some protection from the wolf if he should make an appearance along the way.

"This way," said the smallest pig, heading off through the woods, wagging his curly tail behind him. The girls followed, but it was quite slow going as the pigs made regular little stops to dig into the ground with their snuffling snouts, coming up with tasty roots to be munched upon. Their manners had a lot to be desired as there were constant burps and slobbering sounds.
"Is it much further?" asked Janet after a while.
"Mmm, depends what you mean, further than what?" replied the middle pig chomping on a horseradish root he'd just dug up.

"We'll be passing Little Red Riding Hood's house soon, maybe we can stop for tea, her mother makes the most delicious sandwiches and cream scones," responded the eldest pig.
"Oh that would be nice, I could certainly do with a nice cup of tea," said Jenny.
Little did they realize they'd be needing more than a cup of tea by the time they got there!

It had begun to rain, soft refreshing drizzle at first but turning swiftly into big heavy drops which thundered onto the ground too fast for it to be absorbed, pooling into mini lakes. Now, though the girls were all trying to find shelter, buttoning up their coat collars and pulling on hoods, the pigs were squealing with delight! They were in their element. They insisted on a game of Stuck In The Mud, where Janet lost all her dignity when the largest of the pigs got her unstuck from the lake of muddy water by head butting her so that she lay flat out, face down gulping down a mouthful of disgusting churned mud. It didn't help matters that Jill thought this hilarious and was guffawing with laughter and it took all Jenny's tact and diplomacy to right the situation by which time all three girls, and all three pigs were covered from head to toe in sticky, icky mud!

This then is how they arrived at Red's house. When Red opened the door and saw the state of them she suggested they hose themselves down outside as her mother certainly wouldn't thank them if they trailed mud into the house. The pigs were content to stay as they were and so they left the girls with Red and went on their way having seemingly forgotten all about the dangers of the wolf.

"Here's the hosepipe, do you want me to turn it on?" asked `Red.

"Yes please", chorused the girls.

"Stand back over there then," said Red as she turned on the tap and directed the shower of water over the three girls' heads.

"Ouch that's cold!" yelped Janet.

"Turn round and put your back to it," advised Jenny.

Soon all three were cleaned down but dripping wet.

"I'll get some towels and dry clothes," shouted Red as she dashed indoors.

Jill shook her head from side to side like a dog after a dip in the water.

"Don't do that near me," protested Janet.

"Sorry!" said Jill, moving off to the side.

Red reappeared with a bundle of towels and odds and ends from her wardrobe, "See what you can do with these," she said thrusting the bundle at Jenny.

"Everything's red!" said Jenny.

"Of course," said Red, "I have to live up to my name!"

Soon the three girls were toweled dry and dressed in Red's assorted clothes. Jenny insisted on taking the red cloak as the dresses were all far too short for her and she wanted to cover up. Jill had a red bonnet that looked quite cute in a funny kind of way with the little flared red skirt and blouse she'd put together and Janet found a red jumper that had stretched in the wash and served her well as a dress.

"Come along in then, I've told Mother we have visitors so she's put some scones in the oven to bake, they shouldn't take long."

Red's mother was bustling about in her pinny, making the tea, tipping out jam and cream into little pots, arranging cups, saucers and little plates with dainty knives; Jenny offered to help but was told to sit and take her breath, she'd need it later, which Jenny wasn't too sure what was being referred to but accepted gladly.

There was a lovely home baking smell as the scones rose to perfection and were lifted out to rest on a wire rack. The girls were busy telling their story and filling Red and her mother in on their adventure so far.

"Well dears, it sounds as though you're doing a good thing by making things right with the Giantess but I'm not sure how you'll find her."

"We thought we might take her some gifts," offered Janet.

"Oh, that's a good idea, but it'll need to be something big that won't get lost in that ginormous castle of hers," advised Red's mum.

"We thought we'd take her something practical, like a pair of glasses," said Jenny

"I see, then perhaps a trip to town is needed to visit the Snow White Glass factory, they make things to order there, though I'm not sure they've ever had an order for anything on such a large scale."

"It sounds a good place to start, perhaps Red could accompany us," replied Jenny.

"Oh not at this hour my dears, not through the forest, it's not safe. You'd all be best staying here for the night and setting off in the morning, you can go via Granny's and take her a basket of food along the way."

So it was agreed and after a leisurely tea and more chat they retired early to their beds so they could get a good early start in the morning.

The sun shone brightly as they left Red's house carrying a basket full of cookies, apples, bread and cheese for granny. The forest of trees offered a welcome shade from the burning sun and the dappled light held no hint of danger. So it was without a thought that the four girls took a welcome break under what they thought to be a Weeping Willow tree. They were drinking some fresh homemade lemonade when Janet suddenly giggled and said, "Stop it that tickles, silly."

"I'm not doing anything," said Jill, assuming it was her that was being referred to.

"Well someone's tickling me so will they please stop!"

"Alright," came a deep throaty reply.

"Your voice has gone really deep Jenny."

"I never said anything," said Jenny

"Red is it you? You must have really long arms to be reaching me from over there!"

"Not guilty!" Red quickly asserted.

"No, it was me my dear," came the deep voice once more. But this time it was whispered directly into her ear.

Janet got up quickly and looked around and up just in time to see that it wasn't a tree they'd been sitting under but the Big Bad Wolf disguised as a tree.

"Quick, run for it, it's the wolf," she screamed.

There was pandemonium as the girls leaped to their feet and ran for their lives. Fortunately for them the wolf hadn't quite figured on how cumbersome being a tree would make him and it took him quite some time to get rid of the outer part of his disguise and come lumbering after them.

Panting for breath the girls managed to reach Granny's hut and they barred and locked the door behind them.

"Is that you Red? asked Granny.

"Yes Granny, me and some friends," said Red.

"Well come closer and let me have a look at you all," insisted Granny.

So the girls gathered around Granny's bed to let her see them clearly.

"Perhaps your Granny would like some glasses too," suggested Jill.

"What's that dear?" asked Granny, "I didn't quite catch you."

"It's just that we're going into town to get a pair of glasses made for the Giantess so I wondered if we could get you a pair at the same time, then you'll be able to see more clearly and maybe even able to read a book, if you'd like," explained Jill.

"Oh, yes dear, that would be nice," said Granny.

"We can't stop long Granny if we're to get into town and back before dusk so we'll be straight on our way if you don't mind," explained Red. "But once we've gone make sure to lock your door Granny as the wolf was trying to follow us here again and we don't want a repeat of last time do we now!"

"No dear we certainly don't, now you be careful how you go all of you."

So the girls and Red peaked out the door to check the way was clear and no strange looking trees were lurking nearby and then they waved their goodbyes to Granny and went on their way.

Chapter Eight – A Visit to Town

To pass the time on the journey and to keep their fears at bay the girls taught Red a song – FOLLOW THE YELLOW BRICK ROAD – which they sang and danced to amidst gales of laughter as they explained about Dorothy and the land of the Munchkins.

Soon they'd arrived on the outskirts of the city. They could see steeples rising, smoke billowing, skyscrapers towering, the roads were no longer mud tracks but smooth pavemented ways lined with trees of every shape and colour. They found themselves amongst the crowd of happy shoppers browsing idly in shop windows. Jill stared at the window display in Mother Goose's Bookstore, whilst Janet watched the comings and goings from Goldilocks' Hair Salon. Jenny had to promise them they'd come back once they'd sorted out the matter of the glasses. So they crossed through the city with its colourful sights and sounds and finally arrived at the Factory Outlet shop for Snow White's Glassware.

They entered the shimmering showroom where they saw their reflections from every angle, bouncing off the ceiling, coming up from the glass floor, as well as every wall. They were stunned into silence! Jill hardly dared to move for fear of breaking something. Janet suddenly broke the silence with a loud cry, "I don't believe it, come and look over here."
"What is it?" asked Jenny.
"Only Cinderella's glass slippers, look at them, so tiny and slim, so dainty and elegant, I wish I could try them on!" replied Janet.
"Ah, yes," explained Red, "they were made here for the ball of course, the elves did a good job on them, worked extra fast for the Fairy Godmother."

"Will it be elves who make the glasses for the Giantess?" asked Jill

"I would think so," said Red, "they're the ones who do all the special commissions and they're super fast too."

"Right, well let's go and place our order then," said the ever practical Jenny.

Once the order was placed they had time to explore the rest of the town. They were enraptured by the dresses in Sleeping Beauty's Ball-gown shop and had a job dragging Janet out of there. Jill suggested lunch and so they stopped by at Tom Thumb's Pie shop and gobbled down juicy meat pies all round. Then Jenny noticed the Golden Goose Music shop and suggested buying something that made a loud noise so that they could be certain the Giantess would hear them on arrival. They settled on a trumpet.

Soon it was time to collect their order so they returned to the glassware factory to be greeted by a group of dwarves trying to maneuver the biggest pair of glasses imaginable out of the shop door.

"To your LEFT Dopey, your LEFT," shouted one of the dwarves.

"Hold it steady," moaned Grumpy.

"I'm going to snee, snee, sneeze," gasped Sneezy too late.

"This is never going to work," said Doc., "we need help, and there's only one person who can give the type of help we need and that's the Fairy Godmother."

"Bu, but, she'll be frightfully bu, busy and will never agree to come," stumbled Bashful.

" I'm sure when she hears what it's all in aid of she'll be only too happy to help. She likes happy endings after all," said the ever optimistic Happy.

So the Fairy Godmother was summoned from her tower in Charming Castle.

She came flying in with a soft flutter of fairy wings and landed gently on the frame of the glasses.

"You called Dwarves, I hope it's not some trivial problem, I'm very tired after my ordeal with the Ugly sisters and their awful mother."

Jenny was called upon to explain their dilemma and the Fairy Godmother was at once keen to help. With a wave of her wand and a few enchanted words the glasses shrank in size so that they would fit in Jill's rucksack. She then spent a few moments explaining how to wave the wand she gave them and what words to say to restore the glasses to their full size once they were in the hands of the Giantess.

The girls thanked the Fairy Godmother and the dwarves and elves for their hard work and assistance. There followed several handshakes, many hugs and lots of photographs before the girls were ready to go on with their journey.

Chapter Nine – The Last Leg of the Journey

Soon the girls had left the town behind and were once more in the open country, only things began to look different. For a start the trees were taller, the roads were wider, the stones were bigger and flowers appeared to turn their huge heads and follow them.

"It's a bit creepy," said Jenny, "Shall we walk a little faster."
"Said a whiting to a snail, there's a porpoise close behind us and he's treading on my tail," recited Janet, who loved the Alice in Wonderland book and knew all the poems by heart.
"I don't want to worry you but don't look back, the Queen of Hearts appears to be on the march with her house of cards!" warned Jill.
"Let's hope it's not our heads she's after," replied Jenny as she quickened her step with a hop and a skip.

A White Rabbit appeared from nowhere and hopped by Jenny's side muttering, "We're late, we're late, for a very important date!"
"Where are you going White Rabbit?" asked Jill.
"Why to find the knave of hearts who's run off with the tarts again," answered the rabbit.
"Does he do so often?" enquired Janet.
"All the time, I'm afraid he just can't resist a jam tart; but he's not very clever and he always goes to the same place to hide," explained rabbit.
"Where's that?" asked Jill.
"Why the Giant's old house just over the next hill."
"Why does he go there?" Jill asked.
"Well it's so big he thinks we won't find him I suppose," came the reply.
"We're going there too," said Jill, "We want to see the Giantess on behalf of our father and say sorry."
"You'll never get her to open the door, her hearing's not what it used to be," cautioned the rabbit.

"Oh dear, please don't say that, we've come such a long way and we just have to see her now, besides we've had a pair of glasses specially made for her as a present," moaned Janet.

"Well unless you can make a really loud noise I don't think you have a chance," persisted rabbit.

"Are those trumpets the Card soldiers are carrying?" asked Jill.

"Why yes of course," nodded rabbit.

"Well then I have a solution to our problem, they could all play a really loud tune together and wake the Giantess for us perhaps."

"I doubt if the Queen of Hearts would agree to her soldiers being used for such a purpose," pointed out rabbit.

"What if we help in the search for the Knave of Hearts? Would she perhaps agree then?" asked Janet.

"Well she might I suppose, but if you don't find him it will be off with your heads you do realize!" rabbit reminded them.

So the girls faced the difficult challenge of finding the Knave of Hearts before anyone else and handing him over to the Queen of Hearts if they wanted to keep their heads, which they really rather did!

Sure enough as they reached the summit of the next hill a castle, the size of which they'd never seen the like before, appeared. It stood so tall it seemed you could barely see the roof. The smoke from the chimneys appeared to be billowing clouds. The windows were so high up you couldn't see in, unless of course you were a giant. There was an imposing front door the size of a double-decker bus stood on its end, which was firmly shut.

"Well we've made it!" sighed Jenny.

"Couldn't we just post the glasses with a note through the door and then go home," said Janet anxiously.

"Don't be daft we haven't come this far just to duck out at the last minute, besides we owe it to dad," argued Jill.

"No time for arguments, the queen and her soldiers aren't far behind and if we don't want to lose our heads I suggest we get on and search for that Knave of Hearts," said the ever practical Jenny. "Now Jill you go with the White Rabbit that way, and Janet, you and I'll go this way."

They went their separate ways circling the castle. The grass was nearly up to their heads and would be easy to hide in. It would be like looking for a needle in a haystack. Fortunately White Rabbit had been before and seemed to know his way around even though he was much smaller and could obviously see nothing but grass. He paused every so often and sniffed the air.

"This way, this way," he called.

"How do you know?" asked Jill.

"Why the smell of the jam tarts of course." Came the reply as rabbit leapt forward and Jill had to run to keep up.

Meanwhile Jenny was leading a reluctant Janet through the grounds and following a pathway that led through a kitchen garden. There were all sorts of amazing fruits and vegetables. Apple trees hung with apples the size of footballs. Bananas that looked like giant boomerangs. Peaches that made James's giant peach look like a berry! Pumpkins that would need a fork lift truck to carry them. Bean-stalks that appeared to go up endlessly through the sky and beyond. It really was an amazing sight and Jenny wished she had time to linger and explore. But though they searched every corner there was no sign of the naughty Knave.

White Rabbit had got the scent of the tarts now and was hopping and jumping this way and that so that soon Jill was quite exhausted and had to stop to catch her breath. It was then that she heard a gentle sobbing off to her right a little way. She cautiously tiptoed through the grass edging her way closer and closer to the sound. The crying got louder and she parted the grass stalks to see a crumpled card hunched over which seemed to be saying, "Why do I do it, why do I do it," over and over again.

Jill cleared her throat and whispered quietly, "Do what?"
The Knave jumped to his feet, dropping the plate of jam tarts, barely touched, and started shaking from head to foot.
"Please don't let them know I'm here, the Queen will have my head off this time, it was my last warning you see. Oh dear, oh dear, what am I going to do?"
"Ah you've found him I see," said the White Rabbit as he bounded into the grass clearing beside them. "Well done."
"Yes, but I'm not so sure we should hand him over to the Queen," said Jill.
"But you have to. Rush him back to her now and she'll grant you a reward for saving her time in finding him. Then you can ask that the soldiers all play their trumpets loudly," explained Rabbit patiently.
"But he'll have his head chopped off," said Jill indicating the poor Knave who was a sobbing, hiccupping mess by this time.
"Well he shouldn't have stolen the Queen's tarts," came Rabbits sharp retort.

"I think he knows that now," said Jill. "Well Knave, what do you think we should do? You do realize that if we don't hand you over the soldiers will find you anyway and I'll probably have my head chopped off for not doing so."

"I'm, I'm, sorry," sobbed the Knave, "I won't do it again."

"You're right there – you won't have a head to eat with!" Rabbit interjected. This set the Knave off again and earned the rabbit a look of disgust from Jill.

"You might as well take me, I'll be caught sooner or later anyway, I always am!" sobbed the Knave.

"Look I'll see what I can negotiate for you as part of my reward for finding you, I'll ask for your pardon and find some way of putting you out of temptation for the future. How about that?" offered Jill generously.

"Thank you, thank you."

With that Rabbit took one arm and Jill the other and they hauled the Knave to his feet and began walking him back to the front of the house where they could hear the soldiers gathering.

Jenny and Janet had given up on their half of the search and were heading back too. Both parties arrived back at the same time and ran to meet each other.

It was at this point that the Queen noticed them and shouted, "There he is the rascal, off with his head!"

Jill ran forward without thinking and began to explain how she'd found him and thought that there might be a reward in it for her.

"Reward?" exclaimed the Queen, "What kind of reward – not jam tarts I trust!"

"No, no. I just wondered whether we could hear your wonderful soldiers play their trumpets so that we might stir the Giantess into opening her front door to us. You see my sisters and I have a message to deliver and a present we want to give her."

"What present would that be, not my jam tarts I trust!" the Queen seemed to be obsessed with her jam tarts!

"No your majesty, we have had a special pair of glasses made for her and I thought we might offer her your Knave here as a servant to tend to her needs in her old age, I'm sure she'd be most grateful." Jill brought the Knave before her where he stood trembling, waiting to hear his fate.

"Why should I give her anything?" asked the Queen.

"Well if the Knave is here your majesty then he's out of harms way and can no longer steal your precious jam tarts," explained Jill.

"Very good, very good," laughed the Queen.

There was a collective sigh of relief at her laughter and soon everyone present was laughing too.

It was not long before the order was given for the soldiers to line up and raise their trumpets. The White Rabbit was summoned to give the order to play and soon the air was filled with a blaring of trumpets that was so loud the girls had to cover their ears. After a few minutes they turned to see the huge castle door creaking open and there stood the Giantess!

Chapter Ten – Meeting the Giantess

The giantess was a sight to behold. She filled the doorway even though she was quite stooped. Her head was bald, her clothes quite ragged and in need of repair, she was barefoot and her hands were twisted and gnarled.

When the girls turned back to where the soldiers had been they saw them fleeing, along with the Queen and White Rabbit back over the hill as fast as their legs could carry them, only the Knave remained. The girls gripped his hands firmly to stop him running away too.

"Who's there?" came the surprisingly gentle voice of the Giantess.
"Hello, we're sorry to disturb you but we're the daughters of Jack, the little boy who you helped escape from your husband many years ago." Jenny started to explain.
"What was that? Is there anyone there or not, I thought I heard music of a sort, if you can call it that," came back the reply.
"Knave, quickly play something on your trumpet before she goes indoors again," ordered Jill.
The Knave raised his trumpet to his mouth and belted out a lively tune that made the girls want to dance.
"I didn't know you could play so well Knave, well done! It seems to have worked too," said Jill as she rummaged through her rucksack to find the glasses.
"We're down here," she shouted, "and we've brought you these glasses which if you wave this wand over and say, 'REGGIBWORG', 3 times, will GROW BIGGER and allow you to see us."
The Giantess seemed to realize someone was down there below her so she bent low and groped around her. Jill dashed forward and managed to somehow fit the glasses and wand into her wavering claw-like hand.

"Now say 'REGGIBWORG' 3 times, we'll help you," shouted Jill as she encouraged the others to join in and chant, "REGGIBWORG; REGGIBWORG; REGGIBWORG."

Sure enough the magic glasses grew and grew until they fitted neatly over the Giantess's eyes. She looked quite taken aback when she looked around her and finally took in the four little people standing below her.
`"Well I never, look at you little people, what brings you visiting an old woman like me?"
"Perhaps we could come inside and explain," said Janet, "my legs are tired after our long journey."

"Why yes of course, how rude of me, come in, come in."
With that the door was opened wide to reveal a long, wide corridor with paint pealing off the walls and pictures hanging at all angles on rusty nails. The small party ventured forward with Jill leading.
"In here is the coziest," said the Giantess as she led them into the huge kitchen.

"This is just as dad described it to us," commented Janet as she looked around at the huge wall clock, big range oven, massive central table, old rocking chairs, enormous sink, and gaping cupboards.
"How would your father know what it was like?" asked the Giantess.
"Well it's a long story," began Jenny, who went on to tell it all with a few interruptions from Jill and Janet.

"My, my – how nice that he still remembers me after all this time." Said the Giantess once the story had been told.

"Yes and he wanted to come and apologize for killing your husband and causing you all that bother, he was just an adventurous boy back then," Jenny finished.

"Well that's very polite of him, but there really was no need. I never did like the way my husband liked to eat children. Tried to remind him he was a child once, but it didn't bother him, so I fed him up on anything else I could get my hands on – that's why I started the Kitchen garden – tried making him vegetarian, but once he got the smell of meat there was no stopping him. Now how about a cup of tea and some nice jam tarts? I just made them this morning,"

The Knave nearly fell off his stool, "You make j, j, jam tarts?" he stuttered.

"Why yes, they were my husband's favourite, got the recipe from some Queen or other and insisted we had them every week."

With that she reached up into one of the cupboards and brought out the biggest jam tart you've ever seen! One was more than enough for all of them to share. The knave couldn't believe his luck.

"Giantess I wonder if you would care to have me stay and help around the house, I'm very handy with a paint brush and with a needle and thread come to that. Can I offer my services?"

"That would be very nice but I'm afraid I wouldn't be able to pay you."

"I wouldn't want any payment, just board and lodging and a jam tart or two. Consider it payment in kind!" replied a very happy knave.

Everything seemed to be working out just fine and the girls were beginning to think they should be taking their leave when the kitchen door was nudged open and a craggy green nose appeared.

"Oh, Arthur, come on in if you're coming, there's a nasty draught when the door's open,"

Four heads turned to the door to see a long jawed, beady-eyed beast poke his head round.

Janet screamed and jumped out of her chair. The Knave stood on his stool, knees trembling. Jenny curled herself up into a ball. Only Jill was curious enough to watch as a fully-grown dragon entered the room.

"Don't worry dears, he's completely harmless, he's my pet, aren't you Arthur dear? Keeps me company in this big house of mine. Great at lighting the fires too. You can light the kitchen stove now Arthur, it's getting a little chilly in here."

At this Arthur lumbered over to the stove and gently blew a flame setting the coals alight.

"Brilliant!" announced Jill.

The others began to calm down, open their eyes and take in the scene before them. After a while it no longer seemed strange that they were sharing a kitchen with a Giantess and her dragon, who by now had lain down beside her with his head in her lap and was enjoying being petted and fussed over.

Chapter Eleven – Homeward Bound

Soon it would be getting dark and the girls realized they ought to be getting back to their rocket and home. Their dad would be worried sick. They should leave, but now they thought about it they weren't at all sure that they could find their way, particularly in the dark.

When they mentioned this problem the Giantess offered up a solution, "Why Arthur will take you back to the rocket. Plenty of room on his back for three young ladies like yourselves. The flight won't take long and it will do Arthur good to stretch his wings."
"But we wouldn't want to leave you on your own," protested Janet quickly.
"You're forgetting the Knave of Hearts my dear, he'll be keeping me company now."
"Why, yes of course. How exciting, I can't wait," said Jill eagerly.
"Are you sure he knows the way and will it be safe, what if one of us slips off?" came a barrage of questions from Jenny.
"The witch's gingerbread house you said didn't you? Arthur do you know where that is my dear?" asked the Giantess.
Arthur nodded his head, then yawned widely, which sent a shiver from head to toe. With a swish of his tail he was on his feet and ready to go.

Once outside they said their goodbyes and the Giantess helped them mount by picking each of them up very gently in her enormous hands and placing them on the dragon's back. First Jill tucked up tight against Arthur's neck, then Janet, who clutched tightly at Jill's back, and finally Jenny to bring up the rear.
"Now hold on tight and enjoy the flight, you get some really good views from up there, and Arthur go steady and no somersaults, remember you've got passengers on board!" cautioned the Giantess.

With a chorus of goodbyes and frantic waving of hands the dragon opened up a huge pair of wings and gently flapped them up and down building speed as he ran through the grass. Whoosh! They were airborne. Jill whooped with delight, Janet gripped Jill more firmly than ever and Jenny finally decided it was safe to open her eyes.

"Wow, look, the castle still seems bigger than anything, even from up here."

"I know," answered Jill, "isn't it amazing, come on Janet, take a look you'll never get a chance like this again!"

"I'm glad about that, I have no desire to feel this sick ever again," was the reply.

"Oh, please don't be sick down my back, that would be so typical of you"

"Well it would be your own fault for getting us into this situation in the first place," screamed Janet.

"Girls, girls, let's not argue or fight while we're this far up in the sky without seat belts or anything!" said Jenny in a desperate effort to calm things down. Silence fell and Jill contented herself by looking down as they passed over the town that looked like a miniature village from up here. It seemed ages ago that Red had taken them shopping.

It was Jenny who pointed out Granny's little hut in the woods and wondered how she was doing.

"I wonder if Red remembered to give her the glasses we had made for her Granny. I'd like to think she can see who's visiting her and not be fooled by that awful wolf again," commented Jill.

"Oooh look, there's Red's house now and isn't that the three pigs in the field behind the house?" shouted Jenny.

Just then Arthur swooped to the left and for a moment they felt as if they might all slide off. Janet's piercing scream was loud enough to be heard for miles around. It took a while for Jenny to calm her down once they were flying smoothly again.

"You haven't forgotten you've got passengers have you Arthur?" Jill reminded him, "Go steady please, we don't want any accidents. I'm sorry about my sister, she's not a very good traveler, but no need to throw us all overboard!"

Now they were over the forest where the Great Race had taken place, Jill smiled at the memory of Hare's defeated face when he realized Tortoise had beaten him once again.

Leaving the forest behind they saw the sheep filled fields and wondered whether Mary's little black faced sheep was among them or was he back with Mary at last and patiently waiting for her after school.

Arthur suddenly made a yowling sound and started nodding his head up and down in an agitated manner. It was as if he was trying to tell them something, which indeed he was. Jill told her sisters to hold on tight just as Arthur pointed his nose up to the sky. His tail tipped downwards, causing Jenny to slide backwards and nearly fall off. Fortunately, just in the nick of time, the dragon raised the tip of his tail and Jenny was shunted forward once more.

"We're going to die, he's trying to kill us," announced Janet, "I knew it was a bad idea!"

"He's not," said Jill, "he's actually saving us from flying straight into the mountains. If you took your head out of your lap you'd see."

Janet gingerly raised her head and saw they were indeed flying over the mountains that they'd gone through on their outward bound journey. She remembered Spider and couldn't help a little smile flicker across her face. She'd never be frightened of spiders again, nor perhaps of flying on dragons come to think of it. For now that she looked about her she couldn't help but appreciate the beauty of flying like a bird, for so it felt.

Janet recognized the hills where they'd met the Gingerbread Man and grinned at how clever she'd been to cover him in perfume – she hoped it had worn off by now though.

"Look to your right, a ribbon of blue, it must be the river," called Jenny from the rear.

"Oh yes, that means it can't be far now, better get ready for the descent," warned Jill.

Sure enough Arthur took a downward turn as they flew into sight of the gingerbread house coming ever closer. The dragon's wings folded back to aid his slowing down and before they knew it they had gracefully come to land.

"That was amazing, thank you so much Arthur," said Jill as she jumped down.

"Yes, very kind of you, and sorry I was such a bad passenger," added Janet.

"We're all very grateful I'm sure," said Jenny, "but would you mind staying to make sure we get our rocket to take off all right, I'm not sure we have enough fire power."

Arthur nodded his head and blew out a plume of smoke followed by a flickering orange flame.

"I think he's trying to tell us he can fire us up!" said Jill.

"Come on then, what are we waiting for, let's go," said Jenny as she opened the door into the rocket.

They all three stood on the threshold for a moment or two remembering their own precious journey and saying their farewells to this magical land. Then they ducked inside, took up their stations and went through the start up procedure. Arthur added a booster jet of flame power and soon they were airborne once more, but this time set for home.

Chapter Twelve - The Homecoming

The rocket was programmed for the return journey and it didn't take long at all before they re-entered the earth's orbit.

Janet closed her eyes from that moment onwards. The rocket sped over the earth then suddenly it bumped and bounced as it came to land.

Janet cried, "Oh no, we're going to die, help!"

But Jenny reassured her by saying, "No, I think it's okay, we've stopped on the flat ground at least."

"I'll just look out the window to see where we are and make sure we're not on fire," chirped up Jill.

"On fire!" yelled Janet, "We're going to burn to death."

"No, we're not," Jenny cut in before Janet lost her nerve completely, "we're home, take a look out of your window."

Sure enough there was the familiar sight of their dad's workshop.

"Thank goodness, we've made it, we're home, and right back in our garden. I can't wait to get inside, shower and change," said Janet.

"Good idea, you were beginning to smell," Jill whispered, but loud enough for all to hear.

"I expect we all do," put in Jenny. "Look dad's come out of the workshop, let's go and tell him all about our adventure, I expect he's been worried sick."

"You don't think he'll tell me off do you?" asked Jill.

"Only one way to find out," said Jenny, opening the door and jumping down.

Soon all three girls were running across the garden into their dad's outstretched arms. After a big group hug Jack took each of his precious daughters in turn and gave them a hug and a kiss.

"You don't know how relieved I am to have you all back safe and sound," he said through the tears that were beginning to roll down his cheeks.

"Has Jasper survived the journey too?" he enquired.

"Jasper?" asked the girls.

"Yes, your cat, Jasper, I presume he's come back safely too."

"But he didn't come with us," Jenny protested.

"He must have done, he's not been here," insisted Jack.

"Poor Jasper, I wonder where he's got to, he must have wandered off somewhere, I'll miss him terribly, I hope he comes back once he realizes we're home," murmured Janet.

"I'm pretty sure he was on the rocket when you launched it. He'd made himself a nice cosy bed under the tarpaulin at the back and would sleep there while I worked. That was the last I saw of him." With this Jack and the girls went to investigate inside the rocket.

Sure enough there was the tarpaulin scrunched up at the back of the rocket, the girls hadn't even noticed it before. Jill ran over and tossed it to one side but there was no sign of Jasper. Then Janet noticed one of his favourite toys, a soft ratty creature that he liked to chew and pat around.

"Jasper, Jasper," they all tried calling him but he was nowhere to be found.

"Oh dear," said Jack, "looks like he went with you and then wandered off to find food or something while you were off having fun."

"Fun, Fun!" Janet exploded, "It was the most nerve wracking experience of my life!"

"Well most of it was fun," chipped in Jill.

"But we've gone and left Jasper behind up there in Fairy Tale Land," pointed out Jenny. "What are we going to do? Poor thing, he'll be lost and alone, facing all kinds of dangers."

"Well maybe there's only one thing we can do," Jack said thoughtfully.

"What's that?" chimed the girls together.

"Make another trip back to Fairy Tale Land of course, but you're not to go off on your own again, I'll be coming too this time. First though I need to hear all about what you got up to there."

All three girls were a little nervous of what their dad would have to say but equally keen to tell him of their grand adventure. Jenny wanted to let him know that they'd met and thanked the Giantess and hoped to be able to take her father to meet her personally. Janet wanted to tell him of how brave she'd been when meeting the Spider and how she'd overcome her fears and Jill, well Jill wanted to tell him Everything.

Perhaps you'd like to help tell their dad about their adventures or draw some pictures of what they saw on their travels.

I'm afraid you'll have to wait to find out whether Jasper ever makes it home again!

By Ruth Burgess

THE END